Blue

Copyright © 2004 by Philippe Dupasquier
This paperback edition first published in 2005 by Andersen Press Ltd.
The rights of Philippe Dupasquier to be identified as the author and illustrator of this
work have been asserted by him in accordance with the Copyright, Designs and Patents Act, 1988.
First published in Great Britain in 2004 by Andersen Press Ltd., 20 Vauxhall Bridge Road, London SW1V 2SA.
Published in Australia by Random House Australia Pty.,
20 Alfred Street, Milsons Point, Sydney, NSW 2061.
All rights reserved.
Colour separated in Italy by Scanner Services, Verona.
Printed and bound in Italy by Grafiche AZ, Verona.

10   9   8   7   6   5   4   3   2   1

British Library Cataloguing in Publication Data available.

ISBN 1 84270 436 2

This book has been printed on acid-free paper

Blue

Philippe Dupasquier

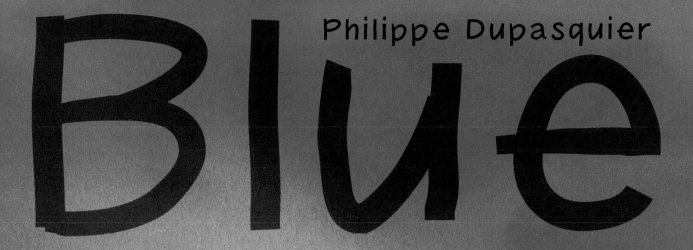

Andersen Press
London

for Sylvie, Tim and Sophie

So we went over to Nigel's. He's got a massive garden and we played football.

First I was in goal,

then it was Simon's turn

and finally Nigel's.

Then nobody wanted to be in goal and we got bored.

Finally we went to see Ricky who has a Scalextric set in his basement.

He's got a 4-lane track with all the latest cars . . .

And a starting grid that smokes when you start – just like a real Grand Prix!

So we decided to go back to mine. But in the street we met up with Sabrina. Sabrina's new. She just moved here. Ricky says she's weird.

"Hi, guys. What are you up to?" she asked.

"Nothing," we replied, "we're bored."

"You can come and play at my house, if you want," she said.

We can have lemonade.

None of us had ever been to Sabrina's house so we said yes.

Sabrina's house isn't like most people's. Her dad's an artist.

"Wow, is that your TV?" asked Ricky.

"Let's play the colour game," Sabrina said. We'd never heard of it!

"It's easy," she explained. "Okay ... For example, today is a good day for BLUE. Come on, I'll show you!" And we followed her upstairs.

We'll go up on the roof. We need LOTS of blue.

We climbed up to the roof and looked out at the view.

Magic! You could see the whole town from here.

"Now, lie on your backs and look straight up," Sabrina ordered.

We did as she said and looked at the sky.

Sabrina was right.
It was blue . . .

"But what are we supposed to do?" asked Ricky.

"Nothing," Sabrina explained.
"Just look at the **blue**."

I told
you she was
bonkers

After a while, Nigel said: "Funny . . . you can hear the whole town but all you can see is blue."

"Every now and again you see birds," Simon added.

"If you scrunch up your eyes
you see loads of things."

"It's like a million blues . . .

no, a zillion blues!"

And then we went quiet for a while. Each of us lost in his

"That's it!" Sabrina cried suddenly.
"The game's over."

We stood up slowly, a bit dazed.
Sabrina grinned at us.

"So, did you like it?" she asked.

You're nuts, Sabrina

Dinner is already on the table. Dad is fuming and even Mum is mad.

I think it best not to argue.

I try to make
myself invisible.
I eat my dinner
as quiet as a mouse . . .
I help clear the table
and finally . . .

All is
forgotten!

Tonight all I can think about is blue.

Tomorrow I'll go and see Sabrina again.
Tomorrow, perhaps . . .

. . . she will show
me another colour.